Jack Sloan in
Tin Star Promise

Agnes M. Hagen

New Readers Press

To my students at Staunton Correctional Center,
who asked for westerns.

Tin Star Promise
ISBN 1-56853-048-X
Copyright © 2001
New Readers Press
Publishing Division of ProLiteracy Worldwide
1320 Jamesville Ave., Syracuse, New York 13210

Printed in the United States of America
9 8 7 6 5 4 3

**Director of Acquisitions and
    Development:** Christina Jagger
Content Editor: Terrie Lipke
Copy Editor: Judi Lauber
Production Director: Deborah Christiansen
Cover Design: Kimbrly Koennecke
Cover Illustration: Luciana Mallozzi
Designer: Kimbrly Koennecke
Production Specialist: Heather Witt

All proceeds from the sale of New Readers Press
materials support literacy programs in the United States
and worldwide.

Chapter 1

The horseman was tired. It was a long ride home from Virginia. Now he just wanted to eat and sleep, but one thing kept him going. Tonight would be different. He wouldn't make camp in some lonely place. Tonight, he would finally be home in Texas. He would be with Molly, his wife, and Tommy, his little boy.

The war was long and bloody, but now at last it was over. Jack Sloan and his family would raise cattle and plant a garden. They would be happy. They would have more children, too. They might not be rich, but the gold Jack buried before the war would help.

During the War Between the States, Jack dreamed many times of coming home. In his mind, he saw Molly running to meet him. Then he gave his son a big hug. They all sat down at the table and ate Molly's good cooking. There would be meat, beans, and corn bread. She would even bake an apple pie. Later, they would sit by the warm fire and tell stories. He would talk about the war. Molly would tell him about home and his son. But that was all just a dream.

Up ahead, Jack saw the little house. He was getting closer and closer. No smoke rose from the chimney. He could see no animals near the house. This was strange. It was a warm day, but now Jack Sloan felt a shiver of cold. Something was wrong!

Riding up to the house, Jack saw footprints and bits of cloth in the grass. Part of a broken table lay near the cabin door. Where was Molly? Where was Tommy? What happened?

Chapter 2

Jack got down off his horse and walked into the house. It was very quiet. Inside, things were upside down. Molly and Tommy were not there. Jack slumped down in a chair. Where was his family? Who had been here? What were they looking for? Did someone find out about the gold he buried?

Jack got up and walked out to the barn. It was quiet there, too. The animals were gone. When he left for the war, there was a cow to give milk for Tommy. And Molly had a horse to ride to town. Did Molly take the animals and leave? Did somebody steal them? Who could have done this?

Jack went to where he had buried the gold. It was still there. Did robbers come looking for the gold? Maybe Molly and Tommy got away. But what if robbers asked Molly where the gold was and she refused to tell?

Sad and tired, Jack went back into the house. He could not eat or sleep. He could think only of his family. He remembered the fine meals he and Molly had eaten in this house. He thought of the cold nights when they sat in front of the warm fire and held each other. And he remembered the day Tommy was born, right here, in this little house.

Thinking about his wife and son spurred Jack into action. He rode into town to see the sheriff. He had to find Molly and Tommy before sundown.

Jack found Sheriff Brown at the jail. The sheriff said that Indians may have been at Jack's house. He and Jack needed to see Chief Gray Hawk right away. If there were unfriendly Indians around, the

Tin Star Promise

chief would know about them.

Jack and Sheriff Brown rode out to the hills where Gray Hawk and his tribe lived. The Indians were all hard at work. Women cooked over fires and wove baskets and rugs. Men cut wood and stretched animal skins on poles.

Jack and Sheriff Brown went into Gray Hawk's tepee. It was dark inside, but a fire lit up the chief's face. He had a strong jaw and shining black eyes. Gray Hawk spoke slowly: "I do not know any Indians around here who might have done this. We all get along very well with your people."

Chapter 3

Jack was upset that he hadn't found his family. He and Sheriff Brown rode back to town. Sheriff Brown turned to Jack. "From time to time, we have gangs of bad men around here," he said. "They come to rob banks and ranches or hold up trains. Maybe one of those gangs went to your house."

"If that is true, how can we find out who they were?" asked Jack.

"We can ask if people in town have seen anyone new," said the sheriff. "Why don't you start at the general store? New people often stop there for supplies. I'll go check the train station."

The store was crowded. Ranchers were buying tools and sacks of flour. Ladies were buying cloth and ribbons. Jack saw the pretty young woman behind the counter. He remembered Ann well. She seemed right at home in her father's store.

"Why, Jack Sloan," she said. "It's good to have you home."

"Ann," Jack said. "I need your help. Molly and my son are missing. I'm afraid something has happened to them."

"Oh, Jack, that's awful," Ann said. "They were in here just the other day. Molly and I have become good friends. And Tommy is such a sweet boy. You won't believe how much he's grown, Jack. He's almost four."

Chapter 4

Ann could see how upset Jack was. She tried to remember if she'd seen any strangers lately.

"The only ones I can think of call themselves the Gospel Gang," said Ann. "They are four brothers named Matthew, Mark, Luke, and John. I guess their mama thought they'd turn out better than they did. They came through town just last week. I've heard stories about them. They steal—sometimes even from the poorest folks. They like using their guns, too. They can't be too far away. Let's ask around and see if anybody knows where they were headed."

Ann and Jack talked to the people in the store. Then they went to the saloon and the barber shop. They went to the boarding house, the bank, and the livery stable, but nobody knew where the Gospel Gang had gone. Most people were just happy that the gang had left town without shooting anyone.

The sun was slowly setting as Jack and Ann walked back to the store. Sheriff Brown met them. "I'm going to get up a posse to look for your wife and son, Jack," he said. "We'll leave at sunup. Go home now and try to get some sleep. Tomorrow will be a busy day."

Jack had dinner with Ann and her family, then rode back to his house. He had never felt so alone.

Chapter 5

Jack was up before the sun. He took his rifle and rode into town. Sheriff Brown was there with a posse of 10 men. Jack knew most of them. They all had guns and were on horseback. "We'll head out to the canyon first," said Sheriff Brown. "It's a good place to hide out. The canyon walls are high, and there's fresh water for

Tin Star Promise

making camp."

"Let's follow the river up toward the canyon. We can look for signs of the Gospel Gang or Molly and Tommy," said Sam Turner. The others agreed, so they rode off toward the canyon.

The sun was hot, but there was a breeze. From time to time, the men stopped so that their horses could drink. Suddenly, one of the men gave a shout. "Look over there!" he yelled. "It looks like there may have been a fight!"

Sheriff Brown rode over to the spot. The grass and bushes were matted. Bits of cloth and broken twigs were on the ground. He got off his horse and looked around. "People were here," he said. "I can't tell which way they went. Some tracks look like they head up to the canyon. Others seem to cross the river at the shallow part. Let's split up. Half of you will cross the river with me. Jack, you take the rest of the men and keep going on this side. Come on! Let's find Molly and Tommy!"

Before long Jack's men came upon a cow standing in the water. It was Jack's cow! Maybe Molly and Tommy had been here. Jack spurred his horse faster. He could go back and get the cow after he found his family.

Tin Star Promise

Chapter 6

Sheriff Brown and his men had crossed the river when they saw black smoke in the sky up ahead. "It looks like a fire up there at the Stevens cabin," the sheriff said. "Have your guns ready. There could be trouble."

As they rode toward the smoke, the men saw what was left of the cabin. The fire was almost out. Dead bodies lay near the burned cabin. The whole Stevens family was dead. And Molly's body was there too. Sheriff Brown was sad as he looked at her. It would be hard for him to tell Jack. But where was little Tommy?

"Could Indians have done this?" asked one of the men.

"How could it be Indians?" asked Sheriff Brown. "Chief Gray Hawk is our friend. He and his people wouldn't do something like this. Maybe there are other Indians around who rob and kill. We must find out who did this before they hurt anyone else!"

The sheriff rode off quickly to break the sad news to Jack. The other men would bury the bodies and then try to pick up the trail. They wrapped Molly's lifeless body in a blanket. They put her on one of the horses to bring her to Jack. They knew he would want to bury her at home, where she belonged.

Chapter 7

Jack and the posse were now entering the canyon. The walls rose high around them. Ahead they saw four men sitting around a campfire. "There they are," said Jack. "That must be the Gospel Gang. I don't see Molly and Tommy."

The Gospel Gang reached for

their guns, but Jack's men drew first. They took the guns away from the four brothers. Jack said, "We're looking for my wife, Molly, and my young son. Have you seen them?"

One of the brothers got up and walked toward Jack. "That's Luke," whispered Jack's friend Nate.

"We don't have them," Luke said. "There have been some bad Indians around here. Maybe they have your wife and son."

Luke looked at Jack with a stern face. The other three brothers stared at the fire. They did not say anything.

Then the gang heard Sheriff Brown coming. They all looked up. "Is this a trap?" asked Luke.

"No," said Jack. "The sheriff is my friend. He and some other men are helping me. They must have found something." Jack hoped to see Molly and Tommy, but the sheriff was alone.

Sheriff Brown rode up to Jack. "I'm so sorry," he said. "We found Molly. She's dead, Jack. I don't know who did it. Some other people got killed, too, but we didn't find Tommy."

Nate leaned over to Jack. "I think the Gospel Gang know more than they're saying," he said.

Sheriff Brown nodded toward the Gospel Gang. "They're bad men, but I've never been able to catch them with stolen gold," he said. "They kill the people they rob," he added, "so there is nobody to tell what they did."

Jack looked up. "Sheriff, make them tell us if they know anything. I have to find out who killed Molly. I have to know what happened to my boy!"

Sheriff Brown put his hand on Jack's arm. "I'll do my best," he said.

Chapter 8

Jack spotted something shiny on Luke's belt. He got down to take a closer look. It was the gold locket that Molly always wore. He had given it to her on their wedding day. "Where did you get that locket?" he demanded.

Luke's hand went to the locket. "I found it on the trail," he said.

"No, you didn't," said Jack. "You took it from Molly. Did you kill her?" Jack reached for his gun. His face was red with anger.

Now Sheriff Brown jumped down off his horse. He took the locket from Luke and asked, "How did you get this? Speak up, Luke!"

"We heard that Jack had gold buried somewhere," Luke said slowly. "And we knew that he would be coming home soon. We went to find the gold. We asked Molly where it was, but she wouldn't tell. We took her with us to scare her. We thought we could make her talk. We took the kid, too. As we rode toward camp, Indians attacked us. They had just robbed and killed the Stevens family. There was a big fight, and Molly got shot. Then the Indians took off with the boy."

The rest of the sheriff's men rode up to join him. They led the horse carrying Molly's body.

"Which way did the Indians go?" asked Sheriff Brown.

"It all happened so fast . . . ," said Luke.

Jack looked hard at Luke. "I want to know how you got Molly's locket. Tell me why the Indians killed those other people but didn't kill you. Were you working together? We will find those Indians. Then we'll know what really happened!"

Jack's friend Nate tried to calm him down. "Jack, there is nothing more you can do here. This is a sad day. Let me go home with you now. I'll help you bury Molly by that oak tree she loved."

Jack just nodded to Nate. The two men rode off to bury Molly.

The sheriff and some of his men stayed at the canyon to make sure the Gospel Gang didn't get away. A few of the other men rode off to keep looking for Tommy.

Chapter 9

Later, Jack and Nate met the sheriff and his men back at the canyon. As the sun set, Jack and Sheriff Brown sat by the campfire. They talked about their families.

Suddenly, they heard horses. Jack looked up to see who it was. The other men from the posse were coming. Sam was carrying a

Tin Star Promise

child. Jack ran to him. "Tommy!" he cried. "Is it Tommy?"

Sam rode up and handed the young boy down to Jack. It had been a long time, and Tommy didn't know his father. Jack took him in his arms and gave him a big hug. "I'm your father," he said. They both cried a little. At last, Tommy was safe, but where had he been?

"Sit down, Jack," Sam said. "Tommy is all right, but he saw some bad things. He needs you to make him feel safe now.

"We found Tommy with an Indian family. They live far from Gray Hawk's village. The Indians saw the Gospel Gang robbing and killing the Stevens family. Molly was with them. The gang didn't mean to kill her. They were shooting at the Indians, and Molly got in the way.

"The Gospel Gang set the cabin on fire as they left. Tommy was sitting by his mother crying. One of the Indians picked him up and took him back to their camp. They saved Tommy's life, Jack."

"I wish I could thank the Indians for saving my son. But right now we're going home," said Jack, kissing Tommy warmly. "I need to take care of my big, brave boy."

Chapter 10

Some of the posse wanted to hang the Gospel Gang right away. But they waited for Sheriff Brown. He questioned the Indian family and the Gospel Gang one more time. After hearing both sides, he was sure the gang's story was a lie. He arrested the Gospel Gang and took them to the jail.

Jack and Tommy went home. When they got there, Ann came out the front door. She saw Tommy and ran to give him a big hug. "Where's Molly?" she asked. Jack shook his head sadly. "Come in," said Ann. "I came by to help clean up a little. I'll fix a hot supper for you and Tommy."

After supper, Jack put Tommy to bed. Then he and Ann sat down to talk. Jack told Ann about Molly.

"This has been a sad day for you, Jack. I know that you will miss Molly," said Ann. "I want you to know that I'm here to help you and Tommy. It will be hard for Tommy to get used to not having his mother."

"Thank you, Ann," said Jack. "I'll always love Molly. I'm going to need all the help I can get for a while. But I'm glad that Tommy's all right. When I got him back, I promised myself to spend the rest of my life helping people."

Ann saw tears in his eyes. Gently she put her hand on his shoulder.

The next few weeks were hard for Jack Sloan. There was much to be done to make Tommy feel safe at home again. There was the trial for the Gospel Gang. And, worst of all, he missed Molly.

The Gospel Gang was hanged for murder. Jack could finally live a normal life again. He used some gold to buy chickens. Tommy liked to feed them. Soon Jack would teach him to gather eggs. Tommy was eager to help with the chores. Jack was very proud of his son.

Ann kept her promise to help as much as she could. Many times, while Jack was working on his house and garden, Ann would come by. She played with Tommy. Sometimes she brought him clothes and toys from friends in town. She often baked homemade treats like hot biscuits and cherry pies. Tommy really looked forward to her visits.

Chapter 11

A few months later, Jack's old friend Nate was in the saloon. Many men were there, including Sheriff Brown. A tall man in black pushed open the door and walked in. His eyes were cold like stones. They were the eyes of a man who had killed and was not sorry.

A long scar cut across the man's

face. A smaller man in a big brown hat was by his side.

The man in black walked slowly to the bar. "I'll have a whiskey, straight up," he said.

The bartender handed him a glass. The man in black drank quickly. Then he turned around. Everyone could see that he had a gun. They stopped talking.

Men always left their guns at the door of the Gold Nugget. Even the sheriff was unarmed.

"Put all your money, watches, and gold on the tables," said the man in black.

Sheriff Brown inched toward

Tin Star Promise

the door, where he had left his gun. But the man in black saw him and fired. The sheriff fell to the floor.

Everyone put their money and gold on the tables. The man in black stuffed the loot in a sack. His partner kept his gun on the people.

Then the tall man backed slowly toward the door. He tossed the sack over his saddle and got up on his horse. The other man, who looked more like a young boy, got up on his horse, too. They rode away. For a minute, no one spoke. Then everyone began to talk.

"Check on the sheriff! Is he still alive?" someone shouted.

"Let's get our guns and go after those thieves!" yelled Sam Turner.

"We're with you, Sam!" hollered the men.

Nate said nothing. He knelt down beside Sheriff Brown. They had been friends. Now, Sheriff Brown was dead.

A few of the men offered to bury the sheriff's body. The parson came to say a prayer.

Meanwhile, Nate, Sam, and the others went after the killers.

Chapter 12

In the hills outside of town, two horsemen rode up to a cave. The first rider got off his horse and carried a sack into the cave. The second rider took off a big brown hat. He pulled pins from his hair, and it fell down his back in long dark curls. It was a woman! She jumped down from her horse and went into the cave.

The man in black wiped a long scar off his face with a wet rag. The woman put her arm around him.

"We did it, Bill!" she said. "But I feel bad about killing the sheriff."

"That doesn't matter, Rose. He is in a better place now," said Bill. "And soon we will be in a better place than this cave. Next we'll try a train job. The train that brings the soldiers' pay for Fort Strong will be here next Friday. We'll make plans tonight. Soon we will be rich."

"I hope so. I don't like this. I don't like it at all," said Rose.

Nate, Sam, and the other men were chasing the sheriff's killers. At a fork in the road, the tracks seemed to stop. Just then, Jack Sloan rode up on his horse.

"I was just in town, and I heard what happened. The sheriff was a good man. If it weren't for him, I wouldn't have Tommy," said Jack. "Maybe I can help you find the men who did this."

"We seem to have lost the trail," said Nate.

"Let's fan out and search now, while the sun is still bright," said Jack. "Look for any signs of a trail, men!"

Chapter 13

Before they rode off, the men saw two horses coming. On one horse was a pretty woman with long brown curls. She had on a bright green dress with white lace on it. A big straw hat shaded her face. Next to her was a tall, good-looking man. He wore a dark blue suit and a new hat. His hair and mustache were black, and his nose

Tin Star Promise

was long.

"Hello," said Jack, and the men tipped their hats to the woman. Nate introduced himself and asked the two riders where they were from.

"My wife and I live up in the hills," said the man. "We're new around here, so we're going into town to get some things."

"We're looking for two men," said Sam. "One man is very tall, dressed all in black. And the other looked smaller and younger. The tall man had a scar across his face, and the younger one wore a big hat. They robbed people in the saloon and killed the sheriff. Have you seen two men like that on your way here?"

"No," said both the man and the woman. "We didn't see anybody on the road." Then they said good-bye and rode toward town.

That was strange, thought Jack. Those people were new and going to buy things, yet they had no wagon. Most people who live up in the hills would stock up on things. The trip into town is a long one. They'd leave for town early in the day so they could get back home before dark. It's already late in the afternoon. *Hmmm . . .*

Tin Star Promise

Chapter 14

"There was something about those two," said Sam. "They said they were new around here, but I have the feeling I've seen them before."

"Nate," said Jack, "have you seen them before?"

"Can't say as I have," said Nate. "But, like Sam said, there's something familiar about them."

"Well, let's see if we can find that trail," said Jack. "The sun will be going down soon."

Meanwhile, the young couple rode toward town. Rose turned to her husband. "That was close," she said.

"I wanted to meet up with them," Bill said smoothly. "Now they won't think it was us at the saloon. Even if they find our camp in the hills, they'll blame somebody else."

"I'm scared! I hate living like this!" cried Rose. "If they catch us, they might even hang us. After all, we killed the sheriff! Maybe the money isn't worth all of this. We could be happy in a little cabin. I just want us to be together."

"You know how much you want to be rich," Bill replied. "We have talked about a big ranch with the finest cattle and horses in Texas. We have come this far. We can't turn back now. Besides, you would not be happy in some cabin with a dirt floor! You would be crying every time you got your hands dirty!"

Chapter 15

The men searched until it was almost dark. Then they headed home. Jack Sloan felt that he had let everyone down. He had found no sign of the killers. The only strangers they saw were those two who lived in the hills.

Jack had promised to spend the rest of his life helping people. This

Tin Star Promise

was the first time he tried to help, and he had failed.

Back in town, Nate sensed Jack's feelings. "Now, Jack," he said, "they had a good head start on us. We did all we could today. Let's go get something to eat."

"You men go on ahead," said Jack. "I'm going to stop by the store to see Ann. She's watching Tommy for me. Besides, that couple said they were going there. Maybe Ann could tell me something about their visit."

As Jack went into the store, Ann looked up from the lamp she was lighting. She told him that Tommy had fallen asleep upstairs. She had tucked him in for the night. Then Jack asked about the new couple from the hills.

"Oh, yes," Ann said. "I remember them. She picked out a pretty bonnet, and he paid for it in gold. Most folks around here use paper money. They seemed nice. The woman talked a lot."

"What did she say?" asked Jack.

"Oh, nothing much," said Ann. "She went on about a big ranch they were going to buy with all their money. I think she was showing off a bit." Ann grinned. "I hope that they spend a lot of their money right here."

"That's all they bought, a bonnet?" asked Jack.

"Yes," said Ann. "I think they were going to dinner when they left here. Why do you want to know about them, Jack?"

"Oh, maybe just because they're new in the area," Jack answered. "Thanks for your help, Ann. And by the way, thanks for watching Tommy. He really looks forward to spending time with you."

"I'll bring Tommy home in the morning, Jack," Ann said. They smiled at each other in the dim light of the store, and then Jack left.

Chapter 16

Jack's friends were already eating at the boardinghouse. "Jack, you haven't lived until you've tried some of this stew," said Nate, licking his lips. "Sit down here." Nate pulled a chair out from the table.

"How'd it go at the store?" Sam asked.

"Ann remembered them all right," said Jack. "The man bought his wife a fancy bonnet and paid for it in gold."

"I thought they were going for supplies," said Nate.

"So they said," replied Jack.

"I still say there's something odd about those two," Nate said.

"She was talking about how much money they have and what a big ranch they're going to buy," added Jack.

"Ann said that they were headed this way at dinnertime. Maybe the cook can tell us something about them."

Jack walked to the kitchen, where a large woman wearing an apron was washing a pile of plates. Jack asked her about the couple from the hills, but she hardly remembered them. "I was so busy feeding all those hungry cowboys out there, I had my hands full."

Jack walked back to the table. "No luck," he said.

"Jack, you haven't eaten a bite," said Nate, pushing a bowl of hot stew in front of him.

"Thanks, Nate," said Jack as he picked up his spoon. "Maybe tomorrow we will get lucky."

Chapter 17

Two days later, Jack Sloan was riding his horse on a cliff high above the train tracks. Far away he could hear the train coming. He could see its smoke in the sky. It was on time, and it was bringing the pay for the soldiers at Fort Strong. Jack liked to watch the train as it went by. It was fun to think of where the train had been and where it was going. Jack found a shady place under a small tree to watch the train.

But something was wrong. There was a big rock on the train tracks just past where the tracks curved!

The train came around the bend and hit the rock. The cars went this way and that way. Some of them rolled over. There was a fire at the front of the train. People yelled as they jumped from the train. They ran from the fire as fast as they could.

Suddenly two people were riding on horseback toward the train. They were riding fast. As they got closer, Jack could see that they had red cloths over their faces and big hats pulled down over their eyes.

Jack quickly rode down toward the burning train. He had to try to help. He saw the masked pair pull out their guns. They went to the trainmen and said something Jack couldn't hear. The trainmen walked back toward one of the cars with the two robbers.

"You there!" Jack yelled, as he grabbed his rifle. They didn't hear him. By now Jack thought that maybe these were the same two men who had killed Sheriff Brown. Maybe he could catch the killers and save the trainmen.

Chapter 18

One of the trainmen slid his hand under his jacket. He pulled out a gun and shot at the robbers. The smaller robber fell to the ground. The tall robber turned to the trainman, but Jack fired first. Jack hit the tall robber in the leg.

"I give up," said the robber, with his hands up. "Don't shoot!"

Tin Star Promise

He dropped his gun and ran to his partner. "Rose," he said. "Are you all right?" He uncovered her face and took off her hat.

"It hurts," she said weakly. "I . . . I would have loved you no matter where we lived," and she closed her eyes for the last time.

Jack was shocked to see that the young robber was the pretty woman he had met on the trail two days ago. Nate and Sam were right. They *had* seen the couple from the hills before. They had seen them in the saloon the day they killed Sheriff Brown. Now some of the men from the train helped Jack tie up the robber and take him to the jail.

Chapter 19

A few days later, Nate and Jack walked to Sheriff Brown's grave. "He was a good man and a friend to both of us," Nate said.

"I know how you feel," said Jack. "I lost friends in the war, and then I lost Molly. I'm glad we got the killers, though." The two men were quiet for a moment.

Then Nate turned to Jack. "You know, we are going to need a new sheriff. You did a great job at the train robbery. What would you think of being sheriff?"

"I'm not sure," Jack answered. "Could I be a good sheriff?"

"I know you as well as anyone around here, and I think you would do us proud," said Nate.

Many people in town agreed with Nate. A few weeks later there was an election to make it official. Everyone came to the ceremony. The mayor handed the jail keys to little Tommy. Then he pinned a bright tin star on Jack's chest.

As Jack turned to face his friends, the star shone in the afternoon sun. "My friends," Jack began. "When Tommy was saved, I promised to spend the rest of my life helping people. I will be here to protect you. You have my word on this." Everyone cheered and clapped.

Tommy was playing with the big ring of jail keys. He looked up at Jack. "Dad, can we go see where you will work?"

Ann added that she'd like to go too. So Jack picked Tommy up in his arms and led the way to his new office.